For Jacob

R. P.

For Jack

C. R.

First U.S. large paperback edition 2005

The Library of Congress has cataloged the hardcover edition as follows:

Platt, Richard.
Pirate diary : the journal of Jake Carpenter / Richard Platt ; illustrated by Chris Riddell. — 1st U.S. ed.
p. cm.
Summary: The fictional diary of a ten-year-old boy who, in 1716, sets off from North Carolina to become a sailor, but ends up a pirate instead.
ISBN 0-7636-0848-3 (hardcover)
[1. Seafaring life — Fiction. 2. Pirates — Fiction. 3. Ships — Fiction. 4. Diaries — Fiction.] I. Riddell, Chris, ill. II. Title.
PZ7.P71295 Pi 2001
[Fic] — dc21 00-065198

ISBN 0-7636-2169-2 (small paperback edition)
ISBN 0-7636-2865-4 (large paperback edition)

2 4 6 8 10 9 7 5 3 1

Printed in China

This book was typeset in Truesdell, Humana Script, and La Figura.
The illustrations were done in ink and watercolor.

Candlewick Press
2067 Massachusetts Avenue
Cambridge, Massachusetts 02140

visit us at www.candlewick.com

Abraham

Will

Ben

Noah

Nick

Pirate Diary

THE JOURNAL OF *Jake Carpenter*

RICHARD PLATT

illustrated by CHRIS RIDDELL

CANDLEWICK PRESS
CAMBRIDGE, MASSACHUSETTS

Contents

Notes for the Reader on Jake's World

Daniel

Saul

Bart

This is the journal of Jake Carpenter.

I begin on the twenty-third day of September in the year 1716.

It is the third year of the reign of our good King George, and the tenth of my life.

FOR AS LONG as I can remember, I have lived in the village of Holyoak, North Carolina. My family came to the American colonies from England. I knew not my mother, for she died when I was yet a baby. My father, a medical doctor, raised me with the help of his two sisters. From them I learned my letters. This was my only schooling.

Now, though, my life is to change, for I am to GO TO SEA! My father wants me to study medicine but believes I should see more of the world first. Thus I am to become a SAILOR — at least for a while.

His plan is that I should join his brother, Will, who is already a seaman. My father sent a letter to the owner of Will's ship, who agreed to take me on the crew.

Now the ship has docked and Will has come to fetch me. He is a fine man. He has the same face as my father, but his hands are larger and rough to the touch. Whenever he is ashore he comes to see us, bringing strange gifts and wondrous yarns. My aunts laugh and call them "when-I-was" tales, for this is how they always begin.

Will has told me of sea monsters, mermaids, and of floating islands made of ice. He has seen a whirlpool, sailed through a hurricane, and escaped from pirates. And soon I am to see all of these things FOR MYSELF.

I write this on my last day at home, for tomorrow I shall return with my Uncle Will to his ship, the *Sally Anne.*

Jake Carpenter.

Ill Fortune Delays Us

Monday 24th

This morn Will woke me before sunup. He bid me fetch my belongings, but laughed out loud when I did. "Fie, man!" he snorted. "Do you think we are going to sea in a tailor's shop?" With this he emptied half the clothes from my bag. Seeing my glum face, he told me they were the clothes of a landsman. (This, he explained, is what sailors call those who are used to a life ashore.) "Such finery is no use on a ship, and there's precious little space aboard to stow 'em."

Thus lightly loaded, we set off at dawn. My father clapped me upon the shoulder, wished me luck, and bid Will take care of me. My aunts both hugged me and dabbed my eyes with their aprons (though they would have better dabbed their own, which needed it more).

The journey to Charleston took us all the day and I most eagerly desired to see the sea. When we arrived I said to Will that I had expected the ocean to be bigger, for I thought I spied the other shore in the distance. "Nay, Jake!" he laughed in reply. "This here is but a wide river. The open ocean is three leagues east and is far too big to see across."

Our inn for the night is a mean and grimy place. Even the straw mattresses are lumpy and dusty.

Tuesday 25th

Today we had some ill luck when we went to join our ship. We were yet two streets away from the quayside when Will stopped suddenly. He gazed up at the masts that towered above the houses. "She's not there," he gasped, pointing upward. "The *Sally Anne*! Her masthead is gone!" With this he dropped his bag and, forgetting me, raced to the waterside.

When I caught up with him, he was sitting gloomily with the harbormaster. He told Will his ship had found a cargo sooner than expected and had sailed on the evening tide. I was sorely disappointed. Forcing a smile, Will said, "Never mind, Jake. Our luck will change." Then the harbormaster added, "*Greyhound* is looking for fit and able men. You could do worse than sign on at yonder inn," pointing out an alehouse, "if you can put up with old Captain Nick!" Will shrugged, "Beggars cannot be choosers."

We found a man from the *Greyhound* sitting in a back room. To my surprise, he asked us no questions but bid us write our names in a book below the names of other members of the crew. Thus it was that by signing my name I ceased to be just the son of a doctor and became a sailor!

We go aboard tomorrow.

1
2
3
4
5
18
17
20
19

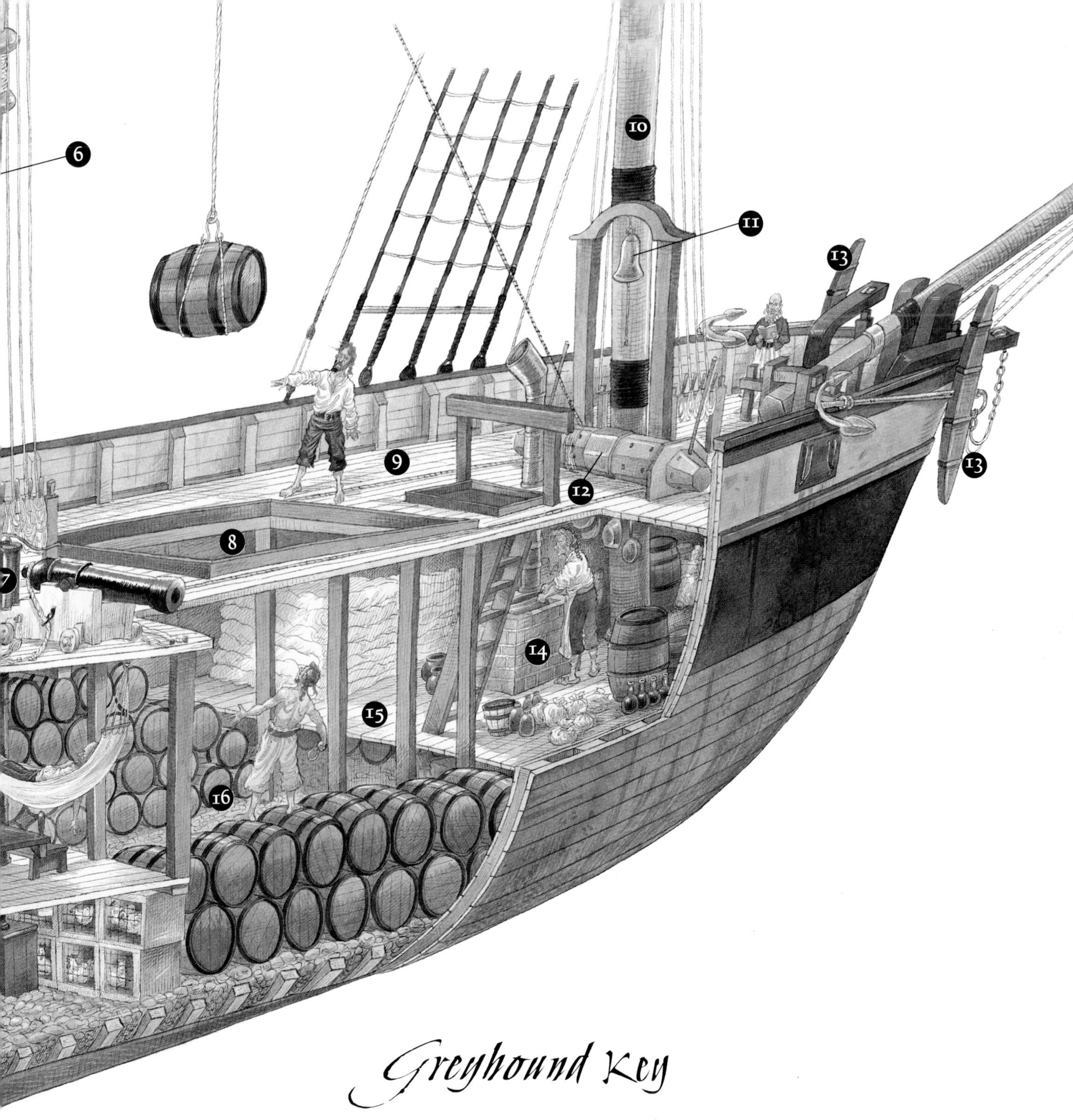

Greyhound Key

1 Tiller
2 Quarterdeck
3 Captain's Sleeping Quarters
4 Great Cabin
5 Capstan
6 Mainmast
7 Pumps
8 Cargo Hatch
9 Upper Deck
10 Foremast
11 Ship's Bell
12 Windlass
13 Anchors
14 Galley
15 Lower Deck
16 Cargo Hold
17 Crew's Quarters
18 Magazine
19 Ballast
20 Stores

I Explore the Ship

Wednesday 26th

This morning Will and I joined our ship. I felt a true landsman, for in walking up the plank from the quayside I lost my footing. Before I could topple into the water, though, Will hauled me on board. One member of the crew saw my misfortune and, when he had recovered from his laughter, led Will and me down into the ship.

Will took down a roll of canvas and, using the ropes at each end, hung it up between two deck timbers. "This hammock is where you shall sleep, Jake. By day you stow it away with your clothes rolled inside."

The *Greyhound* is an odd place. I am to live in a world of wood and water. Almost everything I look upon is wood. That which is not wood is canvas, rope, or tar.

I was thrice tipped out of my hammock before I learned how to climb into it. Now I am here, though, I find it as comfortable as any bed.

I was eager to explore the ship, but before I could do this Will set me to wash the decks. He explained that they must be kept damp, or the boards shrink apart, letting in the sea. This was a long and tiresome chore, but when it was complete I was free to watch the seamen load the cargo.

They did this with the aid of one of the ship's yards (these being the stout beams, crossing the mast, from which the sails hang). Using ropes fixed to yards, it was easier work to hoist the tubs and barrels from the quayside.

There are two tall masts. The front one, which I must learn to call the foremast, has yards for three great square sails. The mainmast behind it likewise has three of these square sails. But behind this mainmast there is also an odd-shaped sail stretched between two spars, making the shape a little like a letter K. I learned that our ship is called a brig on account of this rigging (which is what sailors call the arrangement of the sails, masts, and ropes).

Here I must end, for daylight fades. Candles are permitted only inside a horn lantern, which protects the ship against fire. But it also makes the candle's light into a dull glow that is useless for writing.

Thursday 27th

I already have a friend — the cook's boy, Abraham. He promised me, "I'll make sure your belly is never empty if you learn me my letters." This seemed a good deal to me, but after my first meal yesterday my mind was changed. I had food aplenty, but I could not guess what it was, and ate little of it.

The upper deck of the *Greyhound* I measured today by walking: it is thirty of my paces. At the back, down a couple of steps, is the captain's Great Cabin. At least, I am told it is his cabin, but he has yet to come out of it.

Near the back, beneath the upper deck, is a cabin for the rest of us. This is where we sling our hammocks at night and eat our meals by day, at a table let down on ropes.

The hold in the belly of the ship holds the cargo. I am not allowed to go down there until we are at sea, but from its stink, I guess that we are carrying salted fish. When I ask what is in the hold and where we are bound, Will tells me, "Best not to ask too many questions on board this ship, lad, if you know what is good for you."

My head reels with all I have learned. Every part of the ship has its own strange name. The front is not front, but fore or stem or bows. The back is aft or abaft, or stern, or astern. Right is starboard and left is port (yet some call it larboard, perhaps just to baffle me further!).

Our Ship Sails

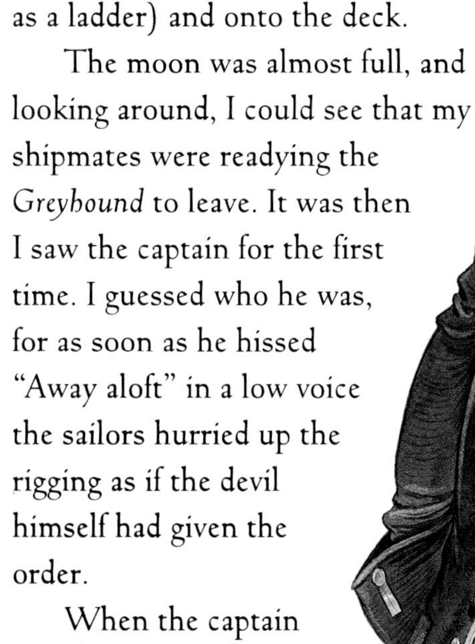

Saturday 29th

In the middle of last night a crewman (it was too dark to see who) pitched me rudely out of my hammock. "Come on, lad, we're getting underway."

Still half asleep, I clambered up the companionway (which is a ship's staircase, as steep as a ladder) and onto the deck.

The moon was almost full, and looking around, I could see that my shipmates were readying the *Greyhound* to leave. It was then I saw the captain for the first time. I guessed who he was, for as soon as he hissed "Away aloft" in a low voice the sailors hurried up the rigging as if the devil himself had given the order.

When the captain glowered at me, I felt a sudden chill, but before he could speak to me, Will beckoned me over. "Jake, jump ashore and loosen the forward rope from yonder bollard. Let it slide into the water — no splash, now — then run aft and jump aboard." It took all my strength to unwind the great rope from the wooden stump on the quayside. The wind pulled the *Greyhound*'s head away from the dock, and I saw why Will had told me to run aft. A yard of water already separated ship from shore and I had to leap to cross the quickly widening gap.

Above us, sailors unfurled the foresail, and it filled with wind. This was enough to make the *Greyhound* glide smoothly away from the dock and into the channel. The tide had just turned, and the current helped us along. Soon we left the harbor lights of Charleston behind us, and as the sun rose over Sullivan's Island we sailed into the open ocean.

Sunday 30th

I discovered this morning why we sailed at night. Captain Nick owes money to Charleston merchants who stocked the ship, and to craftsmen who repaired it. They would have seized the *Greyhound* if we had not slipped away on the tide. He says that when he returns from this trip, he will pay what he owes with interest. However, I doubt the truth of this, for Will has found out that our captain owes the crew three months' wages. "He will keep back ours too," he told me, "to make sure that we stay with the ship."

Abraham at last answered my questions about the cargo. Apart from the fish, all of it is contraband, which is to say, smuggled goods. Smuggling seems hardly a crime to me. It just means avoiding the customs taxes that ships pay to unload their cargo. Abe says, "Even the king's men who search the ship ignore contraband as long as we give 'em a share!" A couple of our shipmates were listening to us talking and one butted in thus: "Why should we Americans pay taxes to an English king who cares nothing about us and gives us no say in the way our affairs are run? So we avoid ports in England or Jamaica where we must pay the customs fees. Instead we unload cargoes in Spanish, Dutch, and French ports in the West Indies and pay nothing."

Our destination is Martinique, where we shall sell the cargo. As I suspected, we are carrying salt fish, but also rice and timber. We will return with sugar, molasses, Dutch gin, French brandy, and lace — all contraband.

OCTOBER Monday 1st

Until today, Will had been looking after me and setting me chores. But as a jest on my family name, the captain has given me as a servant to Adam, the carpenter. I am to help Adam and learn his work. Already he has taught me the names of all his tools so that I can hand them to him when he needs them.

I Learn the Ropes

Tuesday 2nd

Now we are well out to sea the winds and waves are much bigger. Every rope and sail on the *Greyhound* appears stretched to bursting point. Every timber seems to creak and complain, and the seawater licks the deck.

I am very seasick, and suspect that the change of food may not help my guts. We eat mostly a dull stew of beans, with some salt meat and fish and some cheese. The cook told me, "You'd better get to like beans and salty hog, lad. It may be dull but 'tis nutriment enough — and to be sure you shall eat precious little else while we sail."

The cook prepares the food with Abraham in a cabin at the bow of the ship. His hearth there is enclosed in bricks to keep the heat from the ship's timbers.

Ship's biscuits (which everyone calls bread) are as hard as nails. When I first bit into my biscuit, I discovered a dozen little white worms that had made tunnels into it. Abraham helped me. "Eat them in the dark. Or if you cannot wait until nightfall, tap them on the deck. This knocks the worms from their homes."

Wednesday 3rd

Adam sent me to climb to the very top of the mainmast, for as well as helping him I must share in the work of sailing the ship. Abraham came with me as my guide.

Though I have climbed many trees, none was like this. Even in a gentle breeze a mast pitches and sways as if it is trying to shake you off. This made me feel sick with fear, but I tried to hide it lest Abraham guessed my alarm.

Abraham and I have the job of setting and handing the upper topsails (which means letting them down and rolling them up). These are the highest and smallest sails, but they are heavy enough. As we grow stronger we shall move down the mast and set the bigger sails. Abraham tried to teach me the names of each of the ten sails. In return I taught him the names of the twenty-six letters. He learned his lesson quicker than I learned mine.

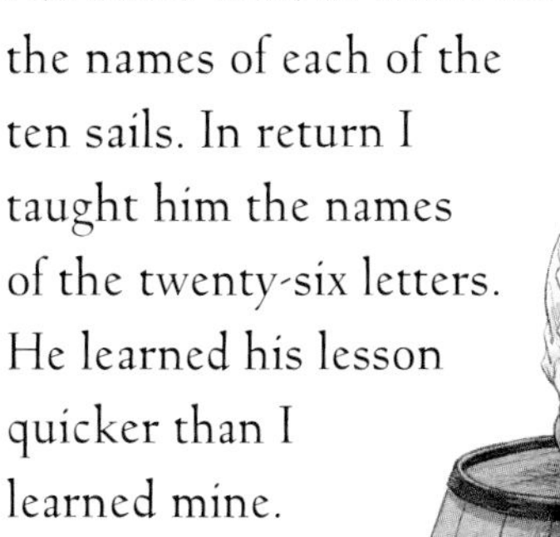

Calmer Waters—and Trouble on Board

Sunday 7th

Since we left port a powerful ocean current has slowed our progress. Noah, our first mate (he commands us when the captain is ill or sleeping), says, "It is like sailing a ship uphill!" Nor has the wind been kind to us. It seemed unsure which way to blow.

At last though, we have sailed into easier waters. The ocean is calmer, and much bluer than it has been until now. The winds are steadier too. This gives us a welcome rest: when the winds change often we must adjust the sails each minute.

Daniel, the second mate, has a goat for milking (which he shares with none but the captain). Today the goat jumped on a cannon and ate our day's bread.

This afternoon, Abraham beckoned to me, hissing, "Jake! Come! The captain sleeps in his bunk and I have sneaked out from the Great Cabin a chart, but make haste, for I must replace it before he wakes." On this sea map he showed me our course and bid me read out the names of places we shall pass by.

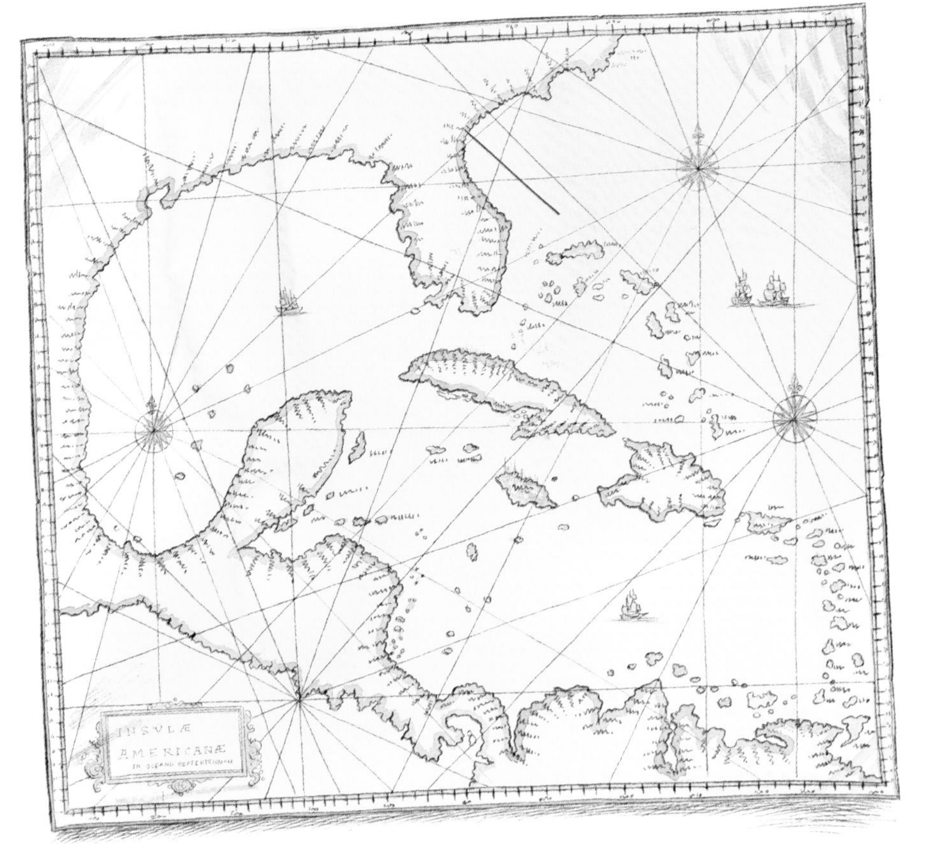

The chart was difficult to read at first, but I eventually found our destination, Martinique.

Monday 8th

Today Adam showed me measuring and marking when we cut out a rotting deck plank and fitted a new one. "Any fool can cut along a line with a saw," he told me. "The clever part is knowing where to draw the line."

Tuesday 9th

The change in the weather and our steady progress have not improved the temper of our captain. This afternoon he spoke only to curse the ship, or d--n the crew, or swear at the wind for not blowing harder.

The only man the captain will listen to is Noah. As first mate, he takes orders from the captain. In truth, Noah manages the ship — and the captain too. He is a skillful navigator. This is to say that he can judge how far the ship has come, and how to steer us onward. All this he tells the captain in his cabin, plotting our course on the chart. When their meeting is over, the captain appears and tells the helmsman in which direction to steer — as if it is he, not Noah, who decides the course.

Wednesday 10th

When Abraham saw me struggling to relieve myself over the deck rail in a strong breeze, he laughed at first, but then grabbed me in alarm, saying, "You will soon be overboard doing that." Then he took me to the ship's waist and showed me the "piss-dale." This is a lead trough that drains into the sea; those using it run no risk of being swept overboard, even in the foulest weather.

Thursday 11th

Saw a man flogged. Captain Nick had been drinking rum until late last night. When he rose, the first man he spied was a seaman working the pumps. (These drain from the hold any water that has leaked in.) The captain judged that he was pumping too slow, and ordered him flogged at sundown.

The poor man's hands were tied above his head to the rail of the quarterdeck. The crew drew cards from a pack to see who would whip him. As luck would have it, one of his friends pulled the lowest card. I guessed he would thus receive a lighter whipping, and at first he did. But seeing that the man held back the whip, the captain ordered him to "Put some effort into it!" Knowing he risked the same punishment if he disobeyed, the poor seaman was forced to whip until his friend's blood sprayed upon the deck. I turned away, but saw those behind me flinch each time the whip came down.

The whip's nine tongues multiply the torment it causes.

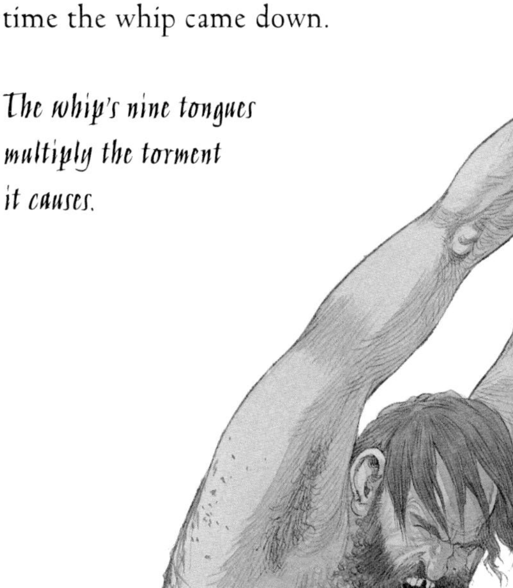

and a heavy plank of wood tied to a length of knotted rope.

Things Go Badly Wrong

Sunday 14th

This day Noah let me see how he navigates the ship. "To get where we want to go, we must know in which direction we sail; and to know where we are, we must know our speed. Direction is easy," he told me, pointing to the compass. "Its swinging needle is magnetic, lad. The earth is like a giant magnet that attracts the needle. The red end always points north, so we can see instantly our bearing, which is where we are headed."

Noah next explained how to measure how fast the *Greyhound* sails. "We heave into the sea a wooden board on a measuring rope. It is marked with knots every forty-eight feet." Noah showed me how to do it. As the floating cord pulled out the rope from a coil I held, I counted how many knots slipped through my hands before sand in a watchglass ran out. I counted four knots, so our ship shall cover four sea miles each hour, or ninety-six in a day. Noah then rules on the chart a line that shows our day's sailing. Its beginning is our position yesterday; its angle is our bearing; its length is the distance we've sailed; and its end is where we are now.

To check his sums, Noah finds our latitude: how far we have traveled north or south. He does this at noon by measuring the sun's height with a machine called a backstaff. "I stare at the horizon through slits at each end," he told me, "then move the block on the smaller arch until its shadow falls upon the slit at the far end." To get the sun's height Noah reads off numbers alongside each slit and adds them. Looking up the total in an almanac — a book of navigator's tables — gives our latitude.

Thursday 18th

I do not want to write of today's evil acts, for they pain me so much. Yet I must, for I mean this journal to be a true and complete record of my voyage.

This morning, while mopping the deck, I lost a bucket overboard. The captain saw this happen and flew into a rage. At first I could not understand why he valued the bucket so highly, but this evening I learned that sailors believe losing one brings bad luck. For me it has proved unlucky indeed.

The captain yelled to the second mate: "Daniel! Flog the stupidity from that idiot landsman or so help me I'll throw him in the ocean!" The second mate dragged me to a cannon and tied me facedown across it.

The crew call him "Do-little-Daniel," for he is the captain's favorite and the only one who dares be seen idle. However, at this task he was most energetic.

I shut my eyes, clenched my teeth, and waited for the rope. But then, suddenly, I heard Will cry, "Stop! Spare the lad, Dan, for God's sake. You'll kill him with that rope!"

For a moment there was nothing but the slap of sail and the lapping of waves. Then the captain's voice. A growl at first, it rose and grew into a terrifying roar. "Do you challenge me, man? Who is the captain here? If this boy is not to pay for his stupidity, then YOU shall — and doubly so."

I was glad I could not see what happened next. I wish I had not heard it, either. My uncle's groans as the rope skinned his back sickened me. After I had counted nineteen lashes he fell senseless. Will's tormentors then bundled him into the skiff, the smallest of our three boats — I heard the splash as it was lowered. By the time I was untied, my uncle was hardly more than a dot far astern. He will surely die without any provisions, and it is all because of my awful clumsiness.

The captain's fury is spent, and my punishment has been reduced from flogging to mastheading. Tomorrow I will be sent aloft and must remain there until summoned.

I Spy a Sail

Friday 19th

Soon after dawn I climbed to the foremast top. I was allowed only some water in a leather bottle to quench my thirst. I was fortunate, for the sea was calm and the sun not strong enough to blister my skin. In fact, my "punishment" was more of a rest than a hardship.

When the morning was half gone, a topman climbed to my perch to reef, or roll up, a sail. He brought from his pocket a hard-boiled egg and said, "Here, Jake, I was cleaning out the chicken coop, and I don't see why Captain Nick should have them all." Later, I got a lump of sugar and an apple (which is a rare treasure on a ship) as other topmen took pity on me.

In the afternoon I thought I glimpsed Will on the horizon waving from his little boat—though perhaps my mind played tricks on me, for by then he would have been far out of sight.

Just before sundown, I really did see another vessel, though the ocean swell often hid it behind the wave tops. As a reward for my sharp eyes I was allowed to come down and was given a bowl of warming soup.

Saturday 20th

With clubs we all hunted rats in the hold, for they eat the cargo, and there was much betting on who would catch the most.

The winner caught nineteen. The lookout saw the ship I first spotted yesterday. She seems to be sailing a similar course to us.

Sunday 21st

Our whole world is turned topsy-turvy! At sunrise this morning the ship was closer and steered toward us. It was flying the Dutch flag. When we came within hailing distance a sailor shouted to us that they needed water. Our captain grudgingly agreed to give them a barrel, for we had plenty, and we shortened sail, slowing the *Greyhound* so that their men could come aboard.

We Are Tricked

I was standing near the bows with Adam as the ship drew closer. "What kind of a vessel is this?" he wondered out loud.

"She has too many guns for her length . . . and apart from the man at the helm there are just three on the deck. Where are the rest of the crew?"

As if to answer Adam's question, one of them forthwith drew a pistol he had hidden in his shirt and fired it into the air. At this signal, the ship's hatches flew open and out rushed a swarm of the fiercest men I have ever seen. All of them carried weapons — short swords, pistols, knives, axes. Each either screamed curses as he ran or uttered a piercing yell. Before leaping aboard our ship, the first of them hurled what looked like a small, round, heavy jug onto the deck. It smashed, and from it burst a puff of gray, foul-smelling smoke. The cloud quickly hid the deck from view, but aloft I could see that the PIRATES (for so they proved to be) had hauled down their Dutch flag, and hoisted a black flag with an hourglass and crossed swords on it.

The pirates' flag.

Their topmen were also hard at work, lashing together the yardarms of the two ships, which were touching.

"Damn your eyes, you treacherous rogues, STOP THEM!" Our captain's voice cut through the smoke and the pirates' yells. "Make sail! Make sail! Steer hard to port!" As the smoke drifted away I could see that the crewmen close by seemed not to hear his words. To my puzzlement they merely stepped back as the pirates boarded.

The first to leap across was a tall, red-bearded man dressed in a fine frock coat. He led a crowd of perhaps twenty pirates toward the quarterdeck. There had been some half-dozen people on it before the attack began. Now all were gone except our captain and second mate. The pair of them had drawn their swords and pistols.

They slashed defiantly at the onrushing crowd, but the fight was too uneven by far. In moments they were surrounded, and their hands tied. But the men tying them up were not the pirates — they were OUR OWN CREW taking them captive!

Nick and Daniel were tied together and imprisoned in the hold.

Monday 22nd

The pirates have taken over our ship. They say it is in better repair than their own, and fast enough until they find a better prize. After the attack, half their number stayed aboard the *Greyhound* and sailed it to an anchorage, where we ride as I write this.

Most of my shipmates are delighted at the ship's capture. As one put it, "Now the flogging will stop." Indeed, this — and fear for their lives — explains why they did all but welcome the pirates aboard.

Bart, the boatswain.

Not everyone is pleased, though. Bart, our boatswain, speaks bitterly of the pirates. Today, as he checked the sails, rigging, and anchor (for these are a boatswain's tasks on the ship), he said to anyone who would listen, "They are just common thieves. Had we not joined them they would have murdered every one of us, yes, as easily as you or I would cut the head off a fish."

Noah argued with him, "That's all very well, Bart, but look at the way old Nick cast Will adrift. Was that not murder too? And is our captain less of a thief? He keeps back half our pay. If we jump ship we have not a penny. Yet if we stay aboard we are slaves."

Bart shook his head at this, but most murmured their agreement with Noah. For myself, I could not decide who was right or wrong. However, I fancy I will not need to choose, for the pirates outnumber us two to one, and they permit no opposition.

In pirates' slang there are one hundred words for "drunk" and just one for "sober."

The Pirates Take Charge

Tuesday 23rd

Today the pirates called all the *Greyhound*'s crew up on the deck and asked about the character and temper of the captain. Nobody spoke well of him, and Thomas, the seaman who had been flogged, showed the weals on his back. Noah urged me forward to tell how my uncle was set adrift. I did not want to speak, for if I had not lost the bucket overboard Will might still be with us. But the pirate captain encouraged, "Come lad, don't be shy. Help us to decide what to do with the captain and second mate. Should we let them take charge again?" This so angered me that I shouted, "NO! Let them suffer the same punishment as my uncle did!"

Despite the discussions lasting most of the day, we are still none the wiser as to what will be done.

Wednesday 24th

We slaughtered and butchered Dan's goat today. It was a stinking nuisance when alive, but the goat's flesh made a fine stew — a welcome change from dried fish and meat. Our cook gave Abraham the skin, and I helped him tie it stretched out tight to dry. He aims to make jerkins for both of us from it.

The pirates have locked away all our weapons, and now sit idly on the deck, smoking pipes, talking, and drinking — which they do to great excess — from a barrel of rum which they took from our hold. Our own crew made willing drinking partners. Bart alone sits apart and clucks his tongue (though even he sneaked a drink from the barrel).

Monday 29th

This day the pirates took from their leaky old tub such sails, ropes, cannon, and equipment as they could easily remove. When all was stripped they fired the ship. The tar-soaked wood blazed down to the waterline. What was left sank with a roar and a hiss.

I can write no more, for we have been told to cut extra gunports in the side of the *Greyhound*, and as Adam's servant I help in this.

Tuesday 30th

Now that we have three times as many people on board, the ship is very crowded. It is worst at night, when the lower deck becomes loud with snores and the air grows thick and heavy. I awoke this morning with a taste in my mouth as if I had slept with a penny in it.

NOVEMBER Sunday 4th

In the short battle to capture the *Greyhound*, a ball from the second mate's pistol found its mark and smashed the shin of Ahab, one of the pirates. Already the wound has maggots and unless his leg is cut off below the knee, he will surely die. All agreed that Adam would make the best surgeon, because he is handy with a saw.

"Shall you help me, Jake?" he asked me. I agreed, but at once regretted it, for he went on to say, "Good, for after I have cut through a vein I shall need someone to press a red-hot poker against it. That will stop most of the blood and keep Ahab from bleeding to death. You can catch the rest of the blood in a bucket."

Though Ahab drank a pint of rum to dull the pain, he howled so loud when the sawing began that I swear the very fish on the sea-bottom must have heard him. Adam was a good choice: he took the leg off in less than two minutes and dipped the stump in hot tar to stop the rest of the blood and help the leg heal. However, Adam now complains that his saw was made to cut wood, and that cutting bone has dulled its blade.

I Am Caught Eavesdropping

Tuesday 6th

Ahab died in the night. Bart sat with him to the end, dabbing his brow. He also read him comforting passages from the Bible, saying that "Even a pirate who is full of sin may be saved."

Methinks that Ahab heard not a word of the Good Book, but his death certainly affected Bart. He now seems less opposed than he was to all of Ahab's shipmates.

Bart sewed up poor Ahab in sailcloth with cannonballs at his head and feet. For the last stitch he passed the needle through the soft flesh between Ahab's nostrils. "That's to make sure he be really dead," he told me, "for the pain of the stitch would surely wake him if he were just asleeping."

Bart read a short prayer, and when all had said "Amen" they tipped poor Ahab into the ocean. The weights in his canvas coffin sank him quickly.

Now we set sail again for Martinique, aiming to sell our cargo there as we had first planned.

Wednesday 7th

When I went below deck this forenoon to fill a bucket with water to wash the deck, I heard voices coming from the stern. The pirates were in the Great Cabin on the deck above. They were discussing what to do with our captain. By standing on a barrel directly below them I could hear every word. One said angrily, "Hang him from the topsail yard? Too kind! Let us slit open his belly."

This made me gasp, and one of them must have heard me, for he hissed, "Hush, someone

listens. . . ." All were silent for a moment. Then to my relief they began again. A softer voice said, "Wicked he may be, and perhaps he deserves to be tortured and killed. But remember, one of us has to do the deed. Jim — you want to spill his guts on the deck. Will it be your knife that opens his belly?"

Again the cabin was quiet, so it was my guess Jim did not want this murderous job. "Well then, unless this man's ill-used crew will do the bloody business, I propose we maroon him."

This last bit I did not understand, but before I could learn more, a big wave tilted the ship and I fell from the barrel with a cry.

I knew from the thunder of feet above that I was discovered. I dived behind some barrels and tried to curl myself out of sight. However, I was soon spotted. "There, over there! There is the scoundrel who dares spy on us!"

The pirates gathered around me in the gloom. Two had their pistols drawn and cocked. A huge and hairy hand lifted me from my hiding place and set me atop a barrel. Someone chuckled. "Why, 'tis the carpenter's lad!"

Stooping, the huge pirate captain brought his face so close to mine that his red whiskers tickled my chin. "So," he whispered, "you have heard what some of us would like to do to your captain?" I nodded. "Well, you wouldn't want to suffer the same fate, would you now?" Before I had time to open my mouth or shake my head, he bellowed, "Then BE OFF with you!" and knocked me from my perch. Thus I escaped, as scared as a rabbit in a snare, but otherwise not harmed.

Our Captain Is Marooned

Friday 16th

Two days ago our ship moored off the shore of a deserted island. The captain and second mate are still tied together in the hold.

We feasted on turtles today, for here they are plentiful. I ate more than was wise, and crept away to my hammock feeling quite ill.

Sunday 18th

We went ashore today to collect fresh water. However, there was a dispute over where we should draw it. Noah, our first mate, wished to look for a spring farther inland. "The water of a spring," he told us, "is always pure. That of a stream is just as clear and tastes as sweet, but a dead animal in a pool upstream can make it unsafe to drink." Ben, the pirate captain, would have none of this, and at his command we fetched water from the first stream we found.

Tuesday 20th

We left the island today, but not before leaving behind the captain and second mate. This is the meaning of "marooning" that I heard the pirates speak of in their meeting.

As the pirates pushed them roughly from the boat into the surf, they handed the two men a musket, some lead balls and a horn of powder. I shrank back, fearing they would load the gun and shoot at us as we rowed from the beach. This made the men pulling on the oars laugh. "Why should they shoot at us?" they asked me. "They shall need every scrap of powder for shooting birds and wild goats to fill their bellies!"

When we returned to the ship we fired off a couple of cannon to celebrate being rid of Nick and Dan at last. One of our crewmen could play the fiddle and he struck up a merry tune while we danced a jig upon the deck.

My new goatskin jerkin makes me look smart enough – but now I smell like Dan's goat!

We Vote for a New Captain

Thursday 22nd

Today we drew water from the barrel we had filled on the island, and those who drank from it soon became ill. The pirate crew called the illness "el vomito" as the Spanish do.

Though we do not have a physician aboard there was no shortage of cures suggested. Abraham had this: "My grandmother always said moss scraped from the skull of a murderer was by far the best cure." Others proposed drinking pearls dissolved in wine or a poultice of pigeon dung. Fortunately we had none of these cures on the ship, and anyway, those who suffered recovered quickly after they had been sick.

Sunday 25th

The life of a pirate is not like that of a sailor on an ordinary ship. There, everyone must obey the captain without question. But this is not so among pirates. The whole company (which is what the pirates call those who sail together on their ship) chooses the captain and other officers. And though the captain commands the ship, the crew may replace him with another if enough disagree with his orders.

Those that fell ill were still aggrieved with Ben's decision on where to draw the water, so today we all picked a new captain. We chose between Noah, our first mate, and the pirate captain Ben. Even though the pirates outnumbered us, Noah was chosen, which pleased me greatly. Ben was a poor loser, and gave Noah an evil look. Though Noah will lead us, the pirates' boatswain, Saul, shall have this same office on the *Greyhound*, for our own boatswain, Bart, is still a most reluctant pirate.

Now we have a larger company and a new captain, the whole crew swore an oath of loyalty. As one of the few crew members who can write, it fell to me to draft the oath. I wrote it in the ship's log, and we all made our mark at the bottom of the page. There were ten "articles" (or rules) to which we swore.

The pirates take these rules most seriously, for they draw them up and agree to them amongst

All those in favor of Noah, raise their hands and say "Aye."

themselves. Many are deserters from the English, French, and Dutch navies. On naval ships, petty rules govern even the smallest things, and sailors are cruelly punished for breaking them. On their own ship (leastways the one they have stolen) the pirates make their own laws, and they respect these above laws made by others.

Noah dictated the ten articles that the company agreed upon and I wrote them in the logbook.

1. EVERY MAN shall obey civil commands.

2. THE CAPTAIN shall have one full share and a half in all prizes; the carpenter, boatswain, and gunner shall have one and a quarter. All others shall have one share.

3. A MAN that does not keep clean his weapons fit for an engagement, or otherwise neglects his business, shall be cut off from his share and suffer such other punishment as the company chooses.

4. IF A MAN shall lose a limb in time of an engagement, he shall have 800 pieces of eight; if a lesser part, 400.

5. IF AT ANY TIME we should meet another pirate ship, any man that signs its articles without the consent of our company shall suffer such punishment as the captain and company think fitting.

6. IF ANY MAN shall attempt to run away, or keep any secret from the company, he shall be marooned with one bottle of water, one of powder, one small arm, and enough lead shot.

7. IF ANY MAN shall steal anything in the company worth more than a piece of eight, he shall be marooned or shot.

8. A MAN that strikes another shall receive Moses' law (39 lashes) on his bare back.

9. A MAN that discharges his pistol, or smokes tobacco in the hold, or carries a candle without the protection of a lantern, or otherwise risks fire on board, shall receive the same punishment.

10. IF AT ANY TIME a man meets with a prudent woman and offers to meddle with her without her consent, he shall suffer death.

An Encounter with a Sea Monster

DECEMBER Monday 17th

Our ship has been sailing against the wind these past three weeks. To make a league's progress forward, we must sail many leagues to port, then go about (which means change direction) and sail the same distance to starboard! Zigzag sailing like this is called "tacking" or "wearing." This last word could not be truer; we are all utterly worn out from working the sails each time we turn.

Tuesday 25th, Christmas Day

I was looking forward to this festival, but I was surprised to find that not everyone on board celebrates this day. To the Dutchmen it was just another day (for *they* celebrate Christmas on January 5th). The English and French sailors made it an excuse for merrymaking and much drinking of rum. Seeing this, Bart said, "You will all burn in Hell's ovens!" He disapproves of such jollity, and marked the festival with several prayers.

JANUARY Wednesday 9th

Last night we all slept not a wink, for we were tortured by a mournful song that seemed to come from the ocean's depths. The sailors on deck could hardly hear it, but the sound echoed plainly through the hull below.

Thursday 10th

During the afternoon the lookout pointed to the starboard side and shouted, "A monster! A great sea monster!"

I rushed to look, and saw the tail of a giant fish thrash at the water, then disappear into the deep. Moments later the beast's gigantic body rose to the surface, and into the air blew a spout of water as tall as two men. The fish was swimming quickly at our ship and I feared it would eat us in a single gulp. But when my shipmates saw my terror, it amused them greatly. One sailor called to me, "Fear not, lad, 'tis only a whale. I've hunted many of these beasts in the icy waters up north." However, at that moment a huge fin appeared from the waves, fully twenty feet in length. It crashed into the ship's side, shaking every timber, and took away a section of deck rail before the beast dived from sight.

We Hide Our Cargo

Saturday 12th

Today we arrived at a small island to careen the ship — that is scraping from her bottom the barnacles and weed that slow our progress through the water. While we are here we shall also repair the damage done by the whale.

First we unloaded the cargo (apart from the disgusting salt fish which remains for the cook to use). From the timber we were carrying we built a stockade. Then we loaded the barrels within it and covered it with old sails taken from the pirate ship. This will serve as our warehouse while we look for a richer prize. To hide it from prying eyes we covered the whole with sand from the dunes.

Next, the *Greyhound* was anchored in shallow water at high tide, and we secured everything on board. When the tide went out the *Greyhound* was left high and dry on the shore and we propped her up with timbers for the work.

Saturday 26th

Careening and repairing the ship has taken these last two weeks. There was much to do so everyone lent a hand, but still it was a tiresome

The loader puts the charge into the barrel, then some cloth to keep it in place, and finally the ball.

The sponger forces them all firmly down into the cannon with a long stick called a "rammer."

The gun captain then cuts the charge by pushing a small spike into the touch hole at the end of the gun.

We were so engrossed in our work the Ranger was nearly upon us before we sighted her.

task. I would never have guessed that so much of the hull lay below the water. After the hull was scraped clean, we coated the ship in a foul-smelling mixture of grease and brimstone, to protect against the plants and tiny sea beasties returning. Adam and I also replaced any broken or rotted planks.

Places to careen a ship are few, for there must be a beach both sandy and steep. So it was no surprise when another pirate ship, the *Ranger*, arrived with the same purpose in mind. This led to some merry carousing, and the story of the sea monster greatly improved in the retelling.

Sunday 27th

We learned from the *Ranger* that a fleet of treasure ships bound for Spain sank off the Florida shore last summer. The Spaniards are using divers to raise gold and other treasure from the wrecks! Everything they find, they carry ashore each night for safekeeping. Pirate leader Henry Jennings is planning an attack on the Spanish camp. The *Ranger* is to join him, and we have agreed to follow!

Monday 28th

We challenged the *Ranger* to a cannon contest today. There was a serious intent behind this sport. Noah wanted to be sure that we could fight as well as we could sail.

Each man has but one job when firing a gun. I am a powder monkey. I run to the lower deck to fetch gunpowder. It is stored there in a "magazine," a cabin protected by curtains of wet canvas against sparks that fly in a battle. Inside, the gunner packs enough powder for each shot into a paper parcel. This we call a "charge."

I take the charge and carry it in a leather box to the cannon. Abraham, who has the same job, warned me, "Be careful! If a spark lights it, the powder will surely blow us both to atoms."

The *Ranger* was the first to hit the target and won the contest. However, our gun crew is the fastest on the *Greyhound*. We can load and fire our piece in less than a minute.

Tuesday 29th

At last we set sail, bound for the coast of Florida, where we shall meet Henry Jennings — and the Spanish treasure!

The gun captain calls, "Run out!" and all eight of the gun crew haul on ropes to pull the gun to the gunport.

The gun captain holds a glowing taper to the touch hole and the ball is fired with a deafening crash.

The Raid!

FEBRUARY Monday 4th

We have reached Florida, and have been joined by three ships. Henry Jennings, who now leads our small army of 300 pirates, calls us "The Flying Gang." A boat rowed him over, and I learned from one of his oarsmen that the three ships come from a place called New Providence, an island only a couple of days' sailing from here. One of our crew who has been there tells me, "It is a paradise, where pirates do as they please without fear of the law."

Wednesday 6th

It was not difficult to find the Spanish as their ships are anchored above the wrecks. The crews sleep ashore, which is scarce two hundred yards distant, leaving a couple of sailors on watch on the ships.

The moon had not yet risen, and we doused all lights except those that shone to seaward. Thus hidden by the night we could sail close in to the shore; so close, in fact, that we could see the fires of the Spaniards' camp and hear the music they were playing. The sailors left on watch must have been drinking too, as they did not espy our approach.

At first, the crew favored leaving me on board the ship during the raid. They thought I was still too much of a landsman to risk on such a venture, but I pleaded with them to take me. Eventually my begging had some effect, for Noah told me he had found me a task. "Very well, Jake. You shall guard the boats on the shore until we return." I guessed that this safe work was chosen because of my age. I did not protest but instead I secretly resolved to follow them to the camp.

With this in mind, I took two pistols that one of the pirates had left behind on his hammock roll. The pistols were too small for the owner's purpose but suited me well, so I hid them in my belt. I was able to load them easily

(I watched how others did it) and powder and ball were free for all before we set off.

Leaving our ships riding at anchor, we quietly rowed ashore. A whistle blast was the signal for our attack. When it came, we sprang upon the Spanish from the shadows. Most fled like frightened rabbits, but not their capitano. He fought so boldly that no one could get near him.

Our boatswain Saul knelt down and aimed his musket at the tall figure now alone in the center of the camp. He pulled the trigger; the flint snapped, the powder flashed, but alas, the gun did not fire. The flash, though, attracted the attention of the capitano.

Saul rose and drew his sword, but lost his footing on the soft sand and tumbled awkwardly to the ground.

In a moment the capitano was on top of him, and stood in his heavy sea boots on the sleeves of Saul's coat, pinning him to the ground. He laughed in triumph as he cocked his two pistols and pointed both at Saul's head.

A blinding flash of light and a deafening blast engulfed me. I had never fired a pistol before, let alone two at once. I was so dazed that I was hardly aware of what happened next. Saul told me that one of my pistol balls flew wide of the mark, but the other hit the capitano's shoulder; thus was Saul's life spared and the capitano quickly captured. His wound was slight, and before we returned to our ships we left him tied to a tree.

Friday 8th

Our attack worked better than any of us dreamed it could. I was a hero (for a day, at least) and was forgiven for "forgetting" Noah's orders to guard the boats and my "borrowing" of the pistols. Without loss of any of our number we captured 350,000 pieces of eight. Henry Jennings counted the coins out into piles on a table in his Great Cabin. He distributed to each his share, but only after taking dice from us, so that we would not gamble it away. For my part I was given 564 of the coins — a small fortune, and more than my father ever had in his life.

I Spy a Mermaid

MARCH Tuesday 12th

Last night I felt more afeared than I ever have since the pirates attacked our ship. Every crew member takes turns on deck watching for danger. I was on middle watch, and thus took my turn in the dead of night. It was cloudy and the sky was black as molasses. As I listened to the creaking timbers, it seemed to me that our ship was alive, breathing and sighing as she pitched in the ocean swell. Worse still, a storm gathered and the upper rigging began to glow with an unearthly light.

I dreaded that the ship was doomed and would be consumed by fire from the sky. I cried out loud, and my alarm brought the gunner (who was also on watch) to my side. He quickly calmed me saying, "Hush Jake, we're all safe. The flames in the rigging are a kind of lightning. There's even a name for them: Saint Elmo's fire." Then he told me that this saint is the guardian of sailors and that I should call on him when I feared harm.

After our successful raid we fled quickly, but now, safe from fear of capture by Spanish warships, most of the crew seem content to do nothing. Adam, however, cannot bear to be idle, so today we went in search of leaks to plug. He called over, "Pass me the Dutch saw, lad; the small 'un." I looked, but could find it nowhere in his bag. We searched the hold and tool store, but the saw had vanished. Adam said, "A wave must have taken it while my back was turned." I worry he does not believe this and suspects that I have lost it — which I have not!

Friday 15th

Today I learned about another of the sea's mysteries. Through the mist we heard a strange chirping song. Then I heard the helmsman gasp, "Look! A mermaid!" Sure enough, there she sat on a sandbank. I had heard of these creatures, half fish, half woman, but I doubted they existed. Now I have seen one, I am still not certain who — or what — they are.

As we all looked, a debate started up. "'Tis a mermaid, no doubt about it," said one. "Nay, man!" said another. "Mermaids are young and beautiful and sit combing their long, blonde hair.

This lass is bald, ugly, and old. Why, she even has long whiskers, and is as big as a carthorse."

I could not decide who was right. I glimpsed her for just a moment, and then the mist hid the sandbank from view.

Tuesday 19th

The other pirate ships having gone on their way, we set sail today for the pirate island in the Bahamas. A misadventure delayed us. Noah is in the habit of leaning against the deck rail and smoking a pipe of tobacco. He always chooses the same spot for this relaxation.

Today, as he rested there, the rail gave way and he plunged overboard. The *Greyhound* was in a flat calm, so we were able to lower a boat and recover him from the water. He was shaken, and the fall had hurt his arm, but he came to no real harm.

Things would have been different indeed had we been under way in a stiff breeze. Then he would have been two leagues astern by the time we had brought the *Greyhound* to a halt.

When we studied the rail we saw it had been cut three-fourths through, and pitch smeared over it to hide the cut. 'Twas clear that it was someone's evil intent the rail break, and not an accident. Noah might have suspected Adam had he not known that the Dutch saw had disappeared a week past.

Since none but the thief knew who had taken the saw, each eyed his companions with suspicion. This is a bad thing on a ship, for the sea is a dangerous place. A hundred times a day you must trust your life on knots your shipmates have tied.

The Pirate's Republic

Friday 22nd

The journey to New Providence is just 200 miles and — aside from Noah's mishap — has so far passed without incident. For the first time since I put to sea I found myself bored.

Some of my companions pass the time by carving sea monsters' teeth into fantastic shapes, or by engraving pictures on them. Adam showed me two coconuts that he had carved and polished to make a drinking cup and a container for tobacco.

Gabriel and Pierre struck up a merry tune on the whistle and fiddle and many of the company danced a jig or two around the deck.

One of the seamen who has hunted whales in the north, passes the time by decorating the skin of his messmates in a manner he learned from the Eskimo people. He pierces their skin with a needle, and pulls a thread rolled in soot through the bloody hole. This looks very painful and I quickly turned down the offer to have myself decorated likewise!

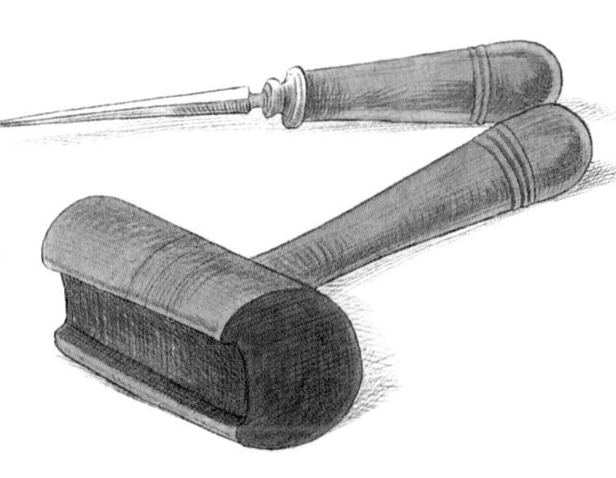

The rope rests in the groove of the serving mallet and is picked open by the fid.

Bart scoffs at all this recreation, calling it "a waste of time." He spends his idle hours sewing clothes for himself and for others who are not as skilled with a needle as he. When he is finished with this industry he carves tools for splicing and covering ropes – that is joining and wrapping them in canvas to protect them. He showed me two: a fid and a serving mallet.

Sunday 24th

We reached New Providence this morning. Within its large harbor are upward of four score ships. We took great care sailing into the harbor, to avoid colliding with the pirates, slavers, and contrabandists moored everywhere.

We handed all the sails, put out the large oars (called sweeps), and carefully rowed the *Greyhound* until we found space to anchor.

It is exactly as I had been told it would be. There are just a few shacks, but the sand dunes have become a town of tents. Their ragged owners sell or rent everything imaginable from ships' provisions and hardware to wine and rum.

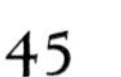

We Hear of an Amnesty

Monday 25th

To go ashore, we had to leap from the rowing boat and wade a little way through the surf. I waited my turn behind Ben (who was the pirate captain until we chose Noah). He jumped into the water, then turned back to get his bag. As he lifted it, something shiny clattered into the boat. I called out, "Wait, Ben! You've dropped something!" We all stared into the bottom of the boat — and there lay the Dutch saw Adam had lost! When I turned to look back at Ben, he had made a run for it. We started after him, but Noah shook his head. "Let him go. We are better off without the rat. I suspected it was he who cut the rail, but as I could prove nothing, I judged it better to say nothing."

APRIL Wednesday 3rd

Today some unexpected news caused great excitement on the island! From a ship out of Bermuda we learn that September last, England's King George declared an Act of Grace, aiming to bring an end to piracy. Those pirates who swear to give up their trade shall receive a royal pardon, and will not be punished. This is good news, since (as is well known) the punishment for piracy is usually execution by the hangman's noose.

The governor of Bermuda had sent his man here to read the Act, and a huge crowd gathered. I could scarcely hear as the wind carried away the man's words. Nevertheless, it was easy to learn what he said, for since then the talk has been of nothing else.

Friday 5th

The pardon has split our company. The navy deserters in our crew oppose it for they say, "Pardon or no pardon, we will be forced once more onto battleships." There are also among us those who hate England's king and despise all his laws and pardons. Some of the company have known no other life but piracy, and others have taken a liking to their new occupation. As one of them told me, "The life of an ordinary sailor, fisherman, or farmer seems a dull one now."

Many of us, though, welcome the king's

The governor's man was scared witless by his audience and sped through his speech.

forgiveness. We all have Spanish silver in our pockets (leastways, those of us who have not lost it at cards among the dunes of New Providence), and a pardon would free us from the fear of capture by the king's men.

However, there is a problem. We need to go to a colonial port to be pardoned. If those who favor a pardon sail away in the *Greyhound*, how shall the remainder go a-pirating? And if the pirates take the ship, how shall the others return?

Wednesday 10th

Our company has reached an agreement. Altogether, those who wish to continue with the piratical life number just ten. The remainder, who want the king's pardon, shall take the ship. In payment for the *Greyhound* each forfeits one fourth of their share of the silver.

I have decided to take the pardon. I fear that if I were to stay a pirate I might never see my father again. And if I were caught and hanged, it would bring great shame on my family.

Parting with a quarter of my share of the Spanish silver seems a high price to pay. However, when we reach our destination we aim to sell the ship, and thus recover our losses.

Friday 26th

Greyhound set sail for Bath town on the Pamlico river. We dare not return to Charleston. Old Nick owed every merchant there money, and we fear they would take the ship in settlement of the debts. Abraham, Adam, Bart, and Noah sail with us, as do thirty others.

I cannot say I am sorry to leave New Providence behind. Some cherish the island as a pirates' paradise, but I shall best remember the stench of the place and the rats (which surely outnumbered the people).

A Great Storm Endangers Us

MAY Saturday 11th

Yesterday, after sighting land, we ran into a storm. Noah had been studying the sky since dawn yesterday, and he had looked uneasy all morning. Just before noon he commanded abruptly, "Shorten sail!"

This surprised us, for the weather seemed fair, with a good following wind. Every one of us was keen to return to shore with all possible haste, but by rolling up the canvas we would sail more slowly. An argument broke out, and Noah was called "a futtock-kneed old fool," but our captain would not be moved.

We went aloft and shortened sail until there were just three sails spread before the wind. However, there was much grumbling on the yardarm, where Noah could not hear.

No sooner had we returned to the deck when the wind veered rapidly round. Half an hour later, we spied black clouds moving in from the east.

"Get the anchor ready! Cook, douse the fire!" cried out Noah. Hearing this, we feared the worst, for clearly he was expecting a sea strong enough to throw the embers from the hearth. "Topmen, shorten sail!" The topmen hurried aloft while on

Shortening sail.

the deck the rest of us hauled the thick anchor cable from its locker. Soon we had only two small staysails set, yet still the wind drove us on through the rising waves faster than a galloping horse. Noah beckoned to a topman standing nearby, and pointed at the sails. "Take some men aloft and hand those last two." Then to Saul, our boatswain: "Stand clear of the cable and let go anchor." Though he was just a few paces away, Noah had to yell the words to be heard above the storm. The anchor dropped into the ocean, and the thick cable snaked from its coils on the deck. It scarcely seemed to halt our progress.

I looked with alarm at the shore, for we were now close enough to see the waves breaking on the treacherous sandbars, and the wind was forcing us closer each minute.

Our brave topmen were handing the last sail when the storm struck. The wind plucked the sail from their hands and hurled it into the foaming ocean. Two of the topmen had lashed themselves onto the yardarm, but the third had not, and he followed the sail into the sea. We could do nothing to save him. By now, each of us had only one thought: to save himself.

Gigantic waves crashed over the deck, shaking the ship as if each one was a great hammer.

The rain had made the yards as slippery as ice, and it was impossible to keep a grip in the howling gale.

I heard Saul shout to Noah, "The anchor's dragging! I'll let go the sheet anchor." This is a reserve anchor, used only in the direst emergencies. But even with two anchors out we were still driving towards the shore.

The ship let out a terrible groan, as if in pain, and there was a mighty crash from above. Looking up, I saw that the storm had snapped the main topmast in two as easily as snapping twigs for kindling, though it is as thick as my waist.

When I saw this I was sure we would all perish, but soon after this catastrophe the storm quieted a little, and then, an hour or so later, it suddenly passed on, leaving the *Greyhound* riding at anchor just a mile from the Carolina shore.

We worked the pumps to drain some of the water that the storm had dashed into the *Greyhound*; Saul also checked and secured what was left of the rigging. Thus satisfied that the ship was safe, we all dragged ourselves to our hammocks, exhausted by the storm. I write these words soon after sunup, while others are yet asleep around me. As soon as they awake, we shall all have much to do if we are to get under way before nightfall.

My Return to Shore

Sunday 12th

We have still not finished repairing the damage done by Friday's storm, but we cannot safely continue until the work is done. The falling topmast brought down with it the upper topsail yards. As it tumbled, this stout timber smashed one of the boats stored on the deck and broke several of the rope stays which hold the masts upright. The boat is beyond repair, but we replaced most of the damaged stays with the spare cordage from the hold. The topmen have spliced together the remainder. Adam and I were kept busy about the deck, making good the smashed rails and other timbers.

The rest of the crew took turns at the pumps. The falling topmast smashed one of the hatches, and thus the sea entered the hold in great amounts. Worse though, the storm so twisted and turned the ship that many seams opened. Without constant pumping the *Greyhound* will founder and sink before the day is out.

Monday 13th

Our repairs are completed today, and we set sail once more. We cannot replace the topmast at sea, but we can spread enough canvas on the yards that remain to make good progress. Noah has decided it is not safe to sail for Bath town port, for it is yet sixty leagues away. Instead, we must return to Charleston, which we shall reach tomorrow, God willing.

Tuesday 14th

By noon today we had sailed up the Ashley River and reached Charleston harbor. As we sailed closer, we saw a grim scene. At the end of the quay, just by the harbor light, stood a crude wooden frame, its timbers bleached white by the sun and sea. Hanging from the frame was an iron cage, shaped like a man. And inside the cage was a man — at least, what was left of a man, though 'twas hardly more than greasy bones wrapped in rags. As I watched, a seagull landed on the cage and pecked at the skull. "It's Jack Rattenbury," said a voice behind me. "He was hanged for piracy two months back. That's a friendly Englishman's way of making an example of those who break their king's laws." After this, we were all silent until the *Greyhound* tied up at the quayside.

The customs searchers were waiting for us. They descended into the ship and had just begun to search the crew's possessions when Noah dropped a purse full of pieces of eight — some ten for each searcher. As none of us stirred to pick up the coins, the searchers guessed that Noah's clumsiness was no accident. Gathering the silver, they cut short their visit. Before stepping ashore, though, they warned us that we should present ourselves at the customs house on Friday to swear an oath of loyalty to the King of England, as the Act of Grace requires.

Friday 17th

Today our company went to the customs house on the quayside. There, each of us stepped up, one by one, before Governor Johnson. A member of his council read the oath from a piece of paper and we repeated the words after he said them. When my turn came, the governor bent down and stared me in the eye. "What's your name, lad?" he asked me. When I told him, he said, "I am most relieved that you have forsworn piracy. You will no longer be a threat to South Carolina or a danger to the good people of Charleston." This remark caused much mirth and laughter.

Every one of us got a letter to prove that we had promised to be pirates no longer, and we returned to the ship. Tomorrow, though, I must seek lodgings. Charleston merchants have got wind of our return and, as we guessed, they have taken the *Greyhound* and will auction her off to get what they are owed.

A Farewell . . . and a Reunion!

Monday 20th

I feel quite alone now, for this morning I bade farewell to Abraham and the others. They have all signed up with another merchant ship and left port today. I was tempted to go with them, until I heard that their cargo is salt fish! I shall miss Abraham especially, for he has been a good friend these last few months.

I shall set off home tomorrow to Holyoak to see my father. He will be most surprised to see me — and my treasure!

Tuesday 21st

This day I had such a wondrous surprise that I cannot believe my good fortune! I had gone for one last look at the *Greyhound*, when I heard someone call out my name. To my astonishment it was my Uncle Will! I had thought him certainly dead, but there he was, as alive as I am.

"I drifted for three days in that little boat, Jake," he told me later, "until fishermen rescued me. The flogging had left my back like a piece of raw meat, but in time it healed." When he was well he had journeyed to Charleston hoping to find work. "I heard that the *Greyhound* was in the port, and came to see if you were still among the crew."

We had much to talk about, and I swear Will did not believe my stories until I showed him this journal and my purse. When we had finished our yarns, we considered whether to buy a farm with my Spanish silver. This we discounted, for we agreed we would miss the sea. I told him of the creek where we had careened the ship, and we pondered whether to sail there and salvage the buried cargo. We rejected this plan too, for the rice was not really ours to claim, and I have left piracy behind me now. Tiredness ended our debate without a decision.

Wednesday 22nd

Will and I have chosen to return home, but then to travel north to join the crew of a fishing ship in Newfoundland. They say you can dip your hat overboard there, and haul it out filled with fish.

My bag is packed and we leave forthwith. Will is shouting for me.

Who knows when I will next have time to continue my journal?

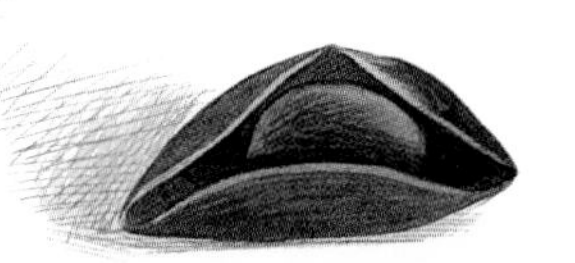

Jake's World

JAKE'S DIARY is a story, but the things he describes are true to life. Seamen really did become pirates to escape from the brutal treatment on merchant ships. But life was tough for landsmen too, and these hardships would bring about some dramatic changes.

The Colonies

Until he went to sea, Jake lived in a tiny village in North Carolina in what is now the United States. In 1716, though, North Carolina was a colony, a region of North America where European people had settled, starting about a century earlier.

North Carolina and South Carolina, where the *Greyhound* departed from, were British colonies. There were eleven others. Each was supposed to be an overseas part of Britain, but the colonists' loyalty to Britain was often weak. Many had fled to America because in England they could not worship as they chose. Others came because the farmland was free or cheap. All of the colonists, though, were independent-minded people with strong ideas.

Life for the colonists was often harsh; cold, hunger, and disease were constant threats. Some were killed by Native American people on whose lands the colonists built their farms. The British also had to fight off rival Spanish colonists. The Spanish wanted the land the British had settled, but the attacks were part of a wider battle. Since the beginning of the eighteenth century, Britain had been at war with Spain and its ally, France.

American colonist

Despite these problems, the thirteen colonies prospered. To make sure that Britain shared in their growing success, the government in London taxed and controlled the colonists' trade. A series of laws, called the Navigation Acts, forced the colonists to trade only with England, using English ships with English crews.

Colonial people did not like the Navigation Acts because the laws forced them to accept low prices for the goods they produced. Many colonists chose to ignore these unpopular laws. They sold their produce wherever they could get the best deal—even if this meant sailing to Caribbean ports occupied by the French. The colonists saw it as fair business dealings. The British government saw it as smuggling.

The people of South Carolina faced special difficulties. They suffered more than most from Spanish attacks because they were closest to Spanish settlements in what is now the neighboring state of Georgia. So they were enthusiastic supporters of the privateers—merchant seamen given permission by the king to attack Spanish shipping and settlements while the two countries were at war.

Peace and Pirates

When Britain and Spain made peace in 1714, the privateers continued harassing the Spanish,

but now illegally, as pirates. Many of the colonists were reluctant to turn their backs on those who had once protected them. They aided the pirates by supplying and repairing their ships. In return, the pirates sold them their booty at reduced prices.

This cozy arrangement worked well — until the pirates' customers tired of their wild manners and violence, and no longer welcomed them in colonial ports and harbors. However, as piracy dwindled, anger about trade restrictions increased. It flared into open rebellion some sixty years after Jake's voyage. In the Revolutionary War that followed, the thirteen colonies broke from Britain, and the United States of America was born.

A History of Piracy and the Lives of the Most Famous Rogues

The First Pirates

When the world's first sailors set off across the Mediterranean some 4,600 years ago, pirates were close behind.

They didn't have to look far. Cautious sailors kept their trading ships in sight of land. This made life simple for pirates, who just anchored close to the shore and waited for a ship to sail into sight.

Viking raider

Viking Raiders

The Mediterranean wasn't the only area threatened by pirates; they also attacked European coasts much farther north. Between the ninth and eleventh centuries, Viking sailors cruised the North Sea, the Atlantic, and the Baltic from their Scandinavian homeland. Traveling in light, fast ships, they raided coastal towns and villages as far west as Ireland, and in the east, deep into Russia. Later, Vikings became settlers, founding peaceful colonies in lands they had once plundered.

Privateers

All these pirates, though, looked like amateurs compared to the rival nations of Europe and their fight for control of the seas. Their kings and queens could not afford to build navies; instead they used merchant ships as "men-of-war"—battleships. These vessels were called privateers, which was short for "private men-of-war." England's King Henry III was the first to use them, against the French, in the mid-thirteenth century. He issued each privateer with a "letter of marque," a piracy permit. This authorized the captain of a merchant ship to attack the enemy on the king's behalf. King and captain each took half the spoils. In practice, many privateers went further. They didn't look too closely to see which country's flag flew from their victims' masts.

When war ended, privateers were supposed to return to their peacetime trade. However, raid and plunder were more profitable, so many privateers carried on in peacetime just as they had in wartime—and became pirates.

Corsairs

Sixteenth-century Mediterranean pirates had a unique excuse for plunder: religion. Three centuries earlier, Christians and Muslims had fought over the Holy Lands—the countries we now call Israel and Syria. Hatred still lingered, and from opposite shores of the Mediterranean, supporters of each religion launched sleek, oared fighting ships called galleys to attack the other's shipping.

Corsair

The Barbarossa brothers

From the Muslim cities of Tunis, Algiers, and Tripoli, galleys went to sea with Christian slaves chained to the oars. The pirates were called "corsairs" after the Latin word *cursus*, meaning plunder. When the corsairs captured Christian ships, they enslaved the crew and passengers. Those too weak to row were taken to work in slave prisons.

Christians launched counterattacks from the island of Malta. Though their religion was different from that of the corsairs, their methods were the same: they used similar galleys, but with Muslim slaves at the oars.

BARBAROSSA BROTHERS
(c.1474–1546)
Of all the Barbary corsairs, none were more famous than the Barbarossa brothers, Aruj (died 1518) and Khayr ad-Din (died 1546). These Greek Muslim pirates made Algiers a powerful corsair base in the early sixteenth century. Khayr ad-Din's exploits earned him promotion from corsair chief to commander of the Turkish navy, and he led raids on many ports in Spain, France, and Italy. The name Barbarossa comes from the Latin words for red (*rossa*) and beard (*barba*).

New World Pirates

As the sixteenth century began, the world grew suddenly bigger. At least, it seemed so for Europeans, whose adventurers discovered a New World on the far side of the Atlantic. Spanish navigators led the exploration of the Caribbean. Moving on to the Spanish Main—mainland America—they plundered the wealth of two great native American peoples, the Incas of Peru and the Aztecs of Mexico. As Spanish treasure ships transported their gold and silver back to Spain by the ton, England's queen sent her privateers to capture them.

FRANCIS DRAKE
(c.1540–1596)
One of England's best-known Elizabethan sailors, Francis Drake, turned pirate after the Spanish raided his merchant ship in the Caribbean. Determined to teach them a lesson, he became a privateer. A 1572 attack on the Spanish town of Nombre de Dios in Panama made his reputation, and a three-year raiding voyage around the world, ending in 1580, won him fame, wealth, and a knighthood from England's queen, Elizabeth I. Sir Francis Drake died of a tropical disease off Panama during his last expedition in 1596.

Buccaneers

When Spain and England made peace in 1604, privateers could no longer legally raid Spanish ships. But before long a new, more brutal breed of pirate appeared: the buccaneers. Originally lawless hunters from Hispaniola (now Haiti and the Dominican Republic), they were named after the "boucan" barbecues on which they smoked their meat. Passing sailors who bought the supplies called the hunters "boucaniers" and later buccaneers.

Hispaniola's Spanish rulers became alarmed by the buccaneers and sent an expedition to shoot all the animals they hunted. The buccaneers got their own back by raiding Spanish ships from their island base of Tortuga. Buccaneer quickly became another word for pirate.

Francis Drake

Britain again went to war with Spain at the beginning of the eighteenth century, and privateers joined the buccaneers in raiding Spanish ships. When peace returned in 1714, they stayed on, and piracy exploded.

FRANÇOIS L'OLLONAIS *(1630–1668)*
French pirate François L'Ollonais was a hunter on Hispaniola when Spaniards attacked his camp, killing his friends. In avenging their deaths, he became the most savage of all the Caribbean buccaneers. In one particularly cruel incident he cut out the heart of one Spanish prisoner and fed it to another. L'Ollonais died as he had lived: captured by cannibals in Panama, he was cut to pieces, roasted, and eaten.

François L'Ollonais

HENRY MORGAN *(1635–1688)*
Henry Morgan became a hero when he led small armies of buccaneers in daring raids on the Central American Spanish cities of Portobello in 1668 and Panama City three years later. Morgan's drunken followers tortured and murdered during the attacks. Nevertheless, the English king, Charles II, later knighted the Welsh pirate for fighting England's enemy, and made him deputy governor of Jamaica!

Henry Morgan

Jake's Adventure

The pirate menace was so great in the eighteenth century that this period is sometimes called the golden age of piracy. This was the world that Jake strayed into when he signed on with the *Greyhound.*

Though Jake never really lived, some of the people he met did. Henry Jennings was a real pirate captain, and his raid on the Spanish salvage crew's camp actually took place. There was even a lawless pirate colony on New Providence—until it was broken up in 1718 by the English former privateer Woodes Rogers. By using the English king's pardon for those who agreed to "retire," Woodes Rogers began a campaign that eventually ended piracy's golden age. In eight years pirate attacks fell from fifty to just six per year.

WILLIAM KIDD *(c.1645–1701)*
When William Kidd sailed from England for the Indian Ocean in 1696, his aim was to capture pirates. His mission was a failure, and, perhaps to satisfy his restless crew, he turned to piracy himself,

seizing the Indian ship *Quedagh Merchant.* Kidd was hunted down, tried, and hanged for piracy. His treasure, though, was never found, and according to legend it still lies buried on a Caribbean island.

HENRY AVERY *(?–?)*
British pirate Henry Avery is famous for a single spectacular—and brutal—raid. Cruising as admiral of a small pirate fleet in the Red Sea in 1695, he sighted the Indian treasure ship *Gang-I-Sawai.* After a fierce battle to capture the ship, Avery and his crew killed and mistreated many of the passengers. The pirates escaped with at least $460,000 worth of gold coins, jewels, and trinkets such as a diamond-encrusted saddle—more than a lifetime's wages for each pirate. Despite a large reward, Avery was never caught.

BLACKBEARD *(?–1718)*
To terrify the crews of ships he attacked, English pirate Edward Teach braided smoking tapers into the long black beard which gave him his nickname. By 1717 Blackbeard's strange appearance, quick temper, and random violence had made him the most feared pirate on America's east coast. He was not the most successful, though, and captured more sugar and cocoa than gold and silver. He died in 1718 in a battle with an English naval expedition sent to capture him.

Blackbeard

MARY READ *(1690–1720)* and ANNE BONNY *(?–?)*
Mary Read and Anne Bonny wore men's clothes when they fought alongside the other pirates on "Calico" Jack Rackham's ship. Whether or not their shipmates knew their true identity is still a mystery. Captured with the rest of the crew, Read and Bonny escaped execution by claiming to be pregnant.

Mary Read & Anne Bonny

JEAN LAFITTE *(c.1780–c.1821)*
Around 1810, glamorous American pirate Jean Lafitte built up a fleet of ten ships off the American coast near New Orleans. Lafitte's gang plundered British, Spanish, and American ships while the United States government was distracted by the War of 1812. Later in the war, Lafitte's pirates helped U.S. forces defend New Orleans against the British foe. To thank him, the president offered to forgive his crimes, but Lafitte rejected the pardon and continued as a small-time pirate until his death.

Jean Lafitte

Piracy Today

Piracy continues today, and those who live by it are as brutal as seventeenth-century buccaneers. Pirates operate in all the world's oceans, but the seas of East Asia are by far the most dangerous — two-thirds of all pirate attacks take place there.

Today's pirates either swoop quickly in fast boats, rob the crew of cash and small valuable items, and then flee, or occasionally they hijack ships to sell not only the cargo but the ship too. And they don't let sympathy for the crew stand in their way. When pirates hijacked the *Global Mars* in the Malacca Straits in February 2000, they forced the crew to flee in an open boat — just as Captain Nick set Will adrift in Jake's story.

Glossary and Index

Page numbers that are underlined show where unusual words that pirates would have used have already been explained. Other unusual words are explained here.

Words shown in *italics* have their own entries, with more information or pages to look up.

A

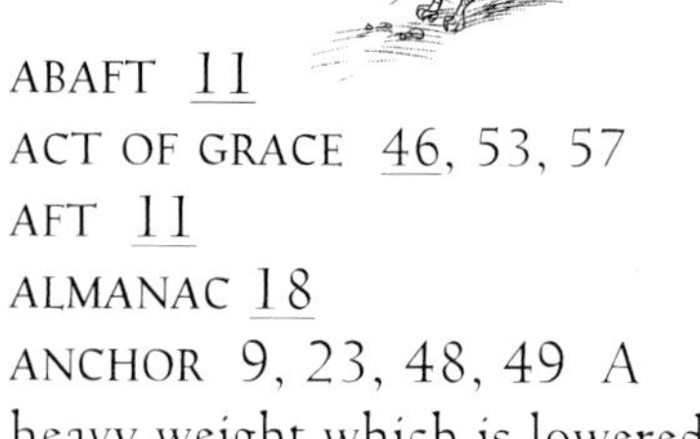

B

C

D

E, F

G

Sources

Writers and illustrators owe a debt of gratitude to the authors and artists whose works inspire them. Richard Platt and Chris Riddell are especially grateful, because they searched in more than forty books for details that would make the text and illustrations of *Pirate Diary* authentic. There isn't room here to list them all, but the following were among the more useful books.

Bayliss, A. E. M.: **Dampier's Voyages**

Botting, Douglas: **The Pirates**

Chapelle, Howard I.: **The History of American Sailing Ships**

Cordingly, David: **Life Among the Pirates**

Cordingly, David (ed.): **Pirates**

Cordingly, David, & Falconer, John: **Pirates, Fact and Fiction**

Esquemeling, John: **Buccaneers of America**

Hall, Daniel Weston: **Arctic Rovings, or the Adventures of a New Bedford Boy on Sea and Land**

Johnson, Charles: **Lives of the Most Notorious Pirates**

Kemp, Peter (ed.): **Oxford Companion to Ships and the Sea**

Mitchell, David: **Pirates**

Rodger, N. A. M.: **The Wooden World**

Stone, William T., & Hays, Ann M.: **A Cruising Guide to the Caribbean**

Willoughby, Captain R. M.: **Square Rig Seamanship**

Inspiration also came from **Howard Pyle**, whose outstanding pirate illustrations have helped fire the imaginations of countless people.

Thanks are due to all of the people who helped and advised us on this project; in particular: **David D. Moore** at the **North Carolina Maritime Museum**, in Beaufort, North Carolina; the staff of **The National Maritime Museum** in Greenwich, London, England; **Alison Toplis**; **David Cordingly**; **David and Kristina Torr**; and **Ken Kinkor** and **Barry Clifford** of **Expedition Whydah**.